For George, Anna, Georgie, Harry, Teddy and Eliza. – Anne Sawan

For my super-talented grandmas, with all my love. I miss you both. – Sernur Isik

First published in Belgium and Holland by Clavis Uitgeverij, Hasselt – Amsterdam, 2016
Copyright © 2016, Clavis Uitgeverij

English translation from the Dutch by Clavis Publishing Inc. New York
Copyright © 2017 for the English language edition: Clavis Publishing Inc. New York

Visit us on the web at www.clavisbooks.com

What Can Your Grandma Do? written by Anne Sawan and illustrated by Sernur Isik

ISBN 978-1-60537-332-4

This book was printed in December 2016 at Publikum d.o.o., Slavka Rodica 6, Belgrade, Serbia

First Edition
10 9 8 7 6 5 4 3 2 1

What can your grandma Do?

Clavis

NEW YORK

Anne Sawan
&
Sernur Isik

"What can your grandparents do?" asked Ms. Appleyard. "Next week is **Grandparents Appreciation Week**. Let's have a talent show, so all your grandparents can share their **special talents** with us."

Everyone cheered — everyone, that is, except for Jeremy. Jeremy loved his grandma, but he **wasn't sure she had any special talent.**

Stella raised her hand. "My grandmother is a doctor. She can show us how to splint an arm."

Jeremy thought about Grandma. She did put ice on his ankle last week after he twisted it playing basketball, but she wasn't really a doctor.

Theo wiggled in his chair and raised his hand. "Oh! Oh!
My abuelo can show us how to paint. He's a great artist!"

Jeremy thought about this. Grandma painted the living room all by herself
after they nicked the wall playing a rowdy indoor game of basketball,
but it was a little streaky in places. And no, *his grandmother wasn't an artist.*

Celeste smiled. "My *Ye-ye* is a **baker**.
I am sure he could make us some **chocolate cupcakes**
with sugar flowers on top."

Aha! thought Jeremy.
Maybe his grandma could do that!
She made **great sandwiches,**
but then he remembered the time Grandma
tried to make a pot roast.

She put the roast in the oven and they
went to play basketball, forgetting all
about dinner until they saw the fire
trucks racing towards their building....

Jeremy shook his head.
His grandma wasn't a chef.

The whole class **buzzed with excitement** as each student shouted out a talent their grandparents could share:

ballet

hula hooping

salsa dancing

making balloon
animals

Everyone except
Jeremy.

"Jeremy," said Stella, "what is your grandmother going to do?"
Jeremy shrugged.

"Doesn't she have any special talents?"
asked Theo. Jeremy looked away.

"What can your grandma do?"
asked Celeste.

Jeremy shrank down in his seat.

That afternoon Jeremy's grandma slid a sandwich under his nose.
"What's wrong, child?" she asked. "You sure are quiet."
Jeremy picked at his sandwich. "We're having a grandparents'
talent show at my school next week."
"Oh, what fun!" said Grandma.

"Yes. Well...
do you have
any talents?"
asked Jeremy.

"Talents? Hmmm, I'm not sure I do," said Grandma.
"Can you juggle?" asked Jeremy.
"I can try!" said Grandma, tossing up
three oranges from the fruit bowl.

"Nope, can't juggle," she said.

"Can you do any **magic tricks**?" asked Jeremy.

"You mean like pull a quarter out of your ear? Let's see."

Grandma gave Jeremy's ear a hard tug. "Ouch!"

"Nothing," she said. "Guess I'm not a magician."

"**Can you cook?**" said Jeremy.

His grandmother gave him a long look.

Jeremy frowned. "Well, what can you do?" he asked.

CRASH!

BASH!

Grandma shook her head
and looked down. "I don't know,"
she said quietly.

Jeremy looked at his grandma, and felt bad.
He knew she had some special talent.
He just knew it... but what could it be?
"Come on, Grandma," he said.
"Let's go play some **basketball**."

"Have you been practicing what I taught you? Watch this!" Grandma said when they got to the basketball court. Jeremy sat and watched as his grandma began to run.

She ran fast.

Then she dribbled the ball, took two giant steps,

leaped into the air, raised the ball towards the rim, and...

Whoosh!

Right through the net... and for
the first time all day, Jeremy smiled.

The next week was the talent show.
All of the students and their grandparents crowded into the gym
and the air was filled with music and the smell of cupcakes.

The excited children learned how to paint and splint broken arms
and do all sorts of wonderful things. Then Ms. Appleyard cleared
her throat. "Class," she said, "Jeremy's grandma is now going
to share her **special talent** with us."

Jeremy's grandma walked slowly to the center of the gym.
Then she began to run. **She ran fast!**

She dribbled the ball,
took two giant steps, leaped into the air,
raised the ball towards the rim
and dunked it right through the net.

The crowd clapped and cheered, and Jeremy turned to his friends.
"Oh yeah, that's right," he said, "my grandma can dunk!"